Walt Disney's
AMERICAN CLASSICS
Johnny
Appleseed

Twin Books

MALLARD PRESS

A long time ago in New England, there lived a boy named Johnny Chapman. Everybody loved Johnny, including the animals of the forest. He led a very simple life, read the Good Book every day and carefully tended his apple orchard because, according to Johnny, "Apples are the finest things on earth!"

From the time he could walk, he had planted apple seeds. And as the seeds grew into trees, so Johnny grew into a fine young man. Nothing bothered him, as long as he had the sun and the rain, the Good Book and his apple trees.

Johnny loved all living things, so wherever he walked, little birds flew about his head, and woodland creatures frolicked at his side. The wildest of beasts trusted Johnny, and would sometimes lie down at his feet to have their heads scratched.

Why, Johnny even loved wolves. Often one would run right up to him. Then, instead of pouncing, that fierce wolf would act just like a puppy.

One day a wagon train rumbled past Johnny's place. "Howdy, young man!" shouted the driver, "C'mon out west with us and be a pioneer!" Johnny wanted to go, but he wondered if it would be wise—he was so comfortable here in the East among his apple trees.

Then, from behind him, a loud voice hollered "JOHNNY!" He turned around, and there stood the most pioneer-looking man he'd ever seen.

"You oughtta go west, Johnny!" said the tall figure. "Shucks, I'm your guardian angel, so I ought to know! I'm here to say that those folks will be needin' apples when they settle out west. What's more, I know you're a real expert at plantin' apple trees!"

Well, the words of his guardian angel made sense to Johnny. The very next morning he was ready to go. He slung a sack full of seeds over his shoulder, plopped an old cooking pot on his head for a hat, and with a seed-planting stick in one hand and the Good Book in the other, Johnny headed west.

Week after week, mile after mile, Johnny traveled west, planting apple seeds over the hills and across the flat plains.

As he went, Johnny was always looking out for folks less fortunate than himself. One time he even gave his shoes to a man who had none. From that day on, rain or shine, Johnny roamed the countryside completely barefoot.

You'd think a man without shoes would have to be mighty fearful of snakes. But they sensed that he loved all creatures, and were grateful when he helped them make their homes in the cool damp earth beneath the trees.

Often, after a hard day's planting, one of the settler families would invite Johnny into their cabin for dinner.

When everybody was through eating, he'd ask, "Would you like me to read a little?" His hosts always nodded yes. When it got too dark to see, Johnny would tell them of the plantings he'd left behind, and in return for their kindness, he'd leave some seeds for them to sow.

Johnny often joined friendly Indians in their teepees for supper or a little chat. As you might guess, he also helped them to plant apple trees.

One day, one of Johnny's Indian friends said to him, "Be careful! My tribe is going on the warpath tomorrow!" Johnny ran all day and all night to warn the settlers. Sure enough, the very next morning, the Indians attacked. No one was hurt because Johnny's warning had sent the settlers to the Army fort.

Shortly after that, a peace treaty was signed and all the fighting stopped. In peace, the Indians and the settlers planted apple seeds together.

Year after year, the seeds that Johnny planted grew into sturdy trees. When the apples were red and ripe, folks came to help with the rich harvest. There were apple pies, apple dumplings, apple fritters and apple cider! All the while, an old-time band played merrily and everybody joined in.

As the years passed, wherever Johnny went, apple trees and good neighborliness sprang up in his footsteps. For Johnny was planting more than apple trees. He was planting his own boundless faith and courage. He gave the settlers new heart and strength to build this great land.

And so it went for forty years, as Johnny Appleseed wandered across the West, looking for places to plant apple trees. No one knows how many trees he actually planted, but they say he popped those seeds in the ground so fast that it somehow looked easy. Settlers who came later heard tales of the kind man with a beard, who had passed by some time before and planted all those beautiful apple trees that awaited them.

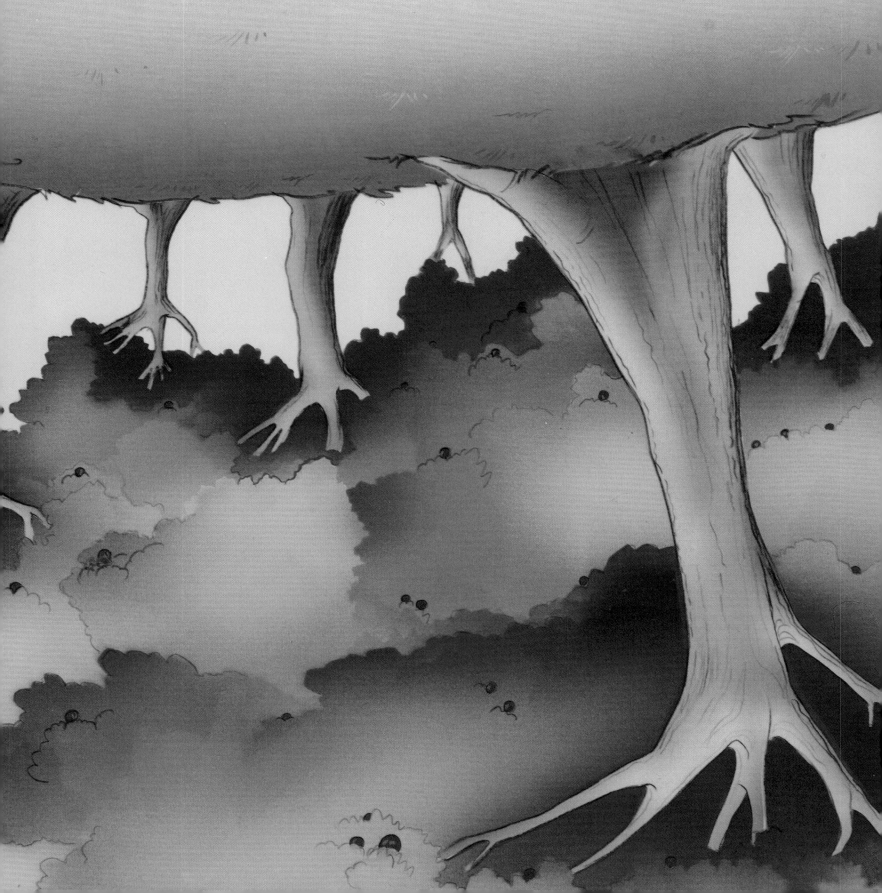

Leaning against one of his trees, Johnny stood off to one side and watched the folks enjoying themselves. He was pleased that the fruit from the orchards had brought them so close together. He reached up and picked an apple off a tree and took a bite. Then with a satisfied smile, he and his animal friends moseyed on westward.

Johnny planted so many seeds on his way to the West that there were apple trees everywhere the settlers looked.

At sunrise and sundown, folks would say, "See that pink color in the sky? Why, that's some of Johnny's apple blossoms glowin' in the sunlight!" After a while, they just plain called that kind of sky an "apple blossom sky."

Johnny wasn't looking for thanks. He figured that if folks saw how the apple trees grew from tiny seeds, it would give them the hope and strength to carry on with what they were doing, and that was thanks a-plenty.

Johnny didn't even stop to notice that he was getting old, and his beard was growing as fast as his apple trees.

As time went by, Johnny's beard sprouted full. The older he got, the longer it got, and the longer it got, the whiter it got.

The whiter it got, the harder it was to tell which was apple blossoms and which was Johnny!

One night, out in the far West, while Johnny was peacefully sleeping under an apple tree, his guardian angel appeared and called to him. "Wake up, Johnny. We've got a mighty long journey to take tonight."

"Now hold on!" said Johnny. "I've got a lot of trees to plant!"

The angel said "That's fine, Johnny. Come home with me—we need a whole lot more apple trees up there!"

Johnny's face lit up with a big smile, and he and the angel left this world behind.

Even now, in the country or in the city, people look up at an "apple blossom sky," and they smile, and think of Johnny Appleseed.

43

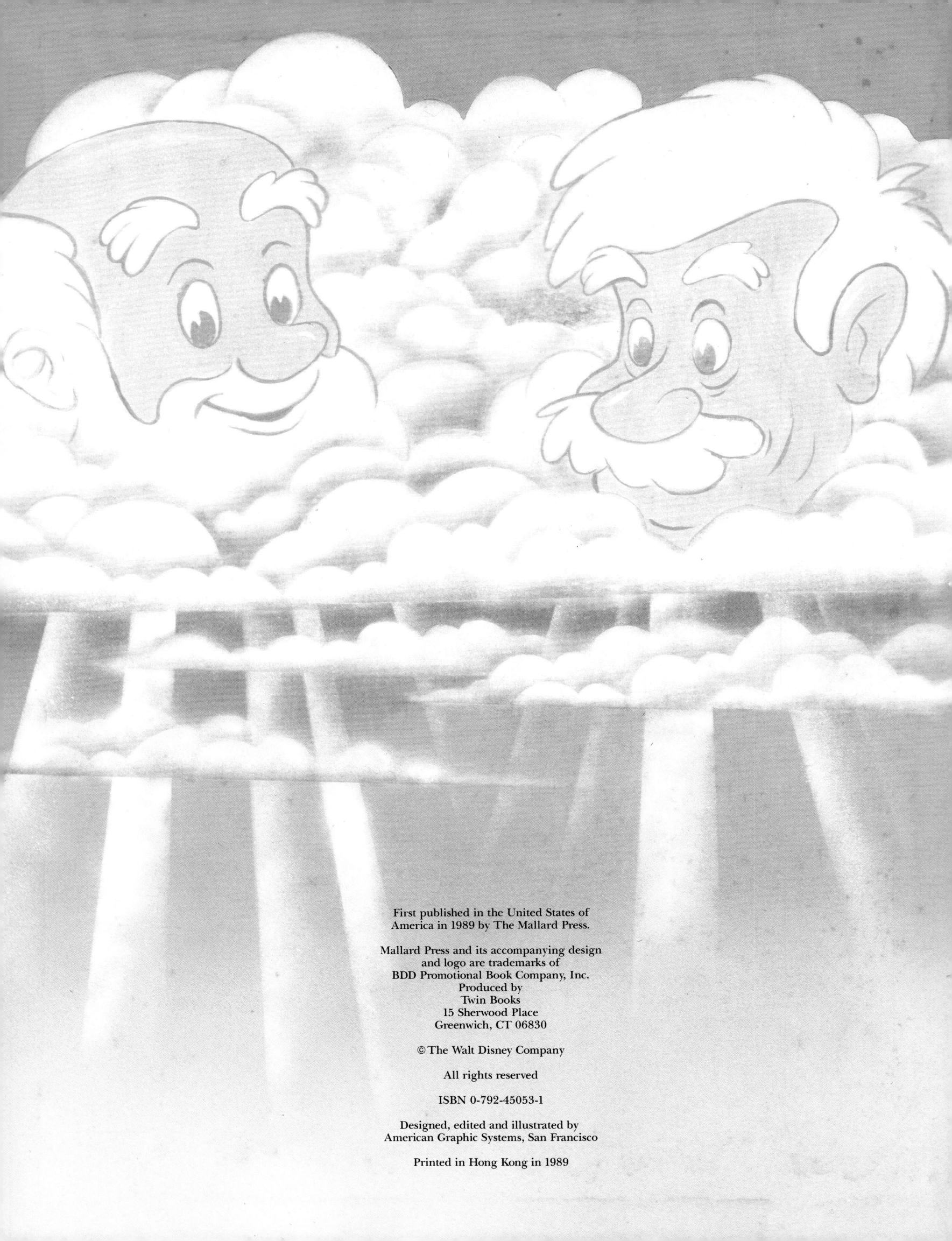

First published in the United States of
America in 1989 by The Mallard Press.

Mallard Press and its accompanying design
and logo are trademarks of
BDD Promotional Book Company, Inc.
Produced by
Twin Books
15 Sherwood Place
Greenwich, CT 06830

ISBN 0-792-45053-1

Designed, edited and illustrated by
American Graphic Systems, San Francisco

Printed in Hong Kong in 1989